POULTRYGEIST

BY
Mary Jane

AND
Herm Auch

Holiday House / New York

**To Mary Cash and
Claire Counihan—
editor and art director
eggstraordinaire!**

Text copyright © 2003 by Mary Jane Auch
Illustrations copyright © 2003 by Mary Jane and Herm Auch
All Rights Reserved
Printed in the United States of America
The text typeface is Barcelona Medium.
All these chickens were created in Photoshop.
www.holidayhouse.com

Library of Congress Cataloging-in-Publication Data
Auch, Mary Jane.
Poultrygeist / Mary Jane and Herm Auch.
p. cm.
Summary: On Halloween night, two rowdy young roosters
encounter a "poultrygeist" in the barn.
ISBN 0-8234-1756-5 (hardcover)
ISBN 0-8234-1876-6 (paperback)
[1. Roosters—Fiction. 2. Domestic animals—Fiction.
3. Poltergeists—Fiction. 4. Halloween—Fiction. 5. Behavior—Fiction.]
I. Auch, Herm, ill. II. Title.
PZ7. A898 Po 2003
[E]—dc21   2001059438

Rudy and his best friend, Ralph, were two rowdy young roosters. They weren't loud on purpose, but there was so much to crow about. Each tried to be the first and loudest to crow at sunrise every morning.

Then they had contests all day long to decide who was the strongest, or the biggest, or the loudest. Finally, at sundown, they wrestled each other for the highest roost in the barn.

Most of the other farm animals didn't mind the racket. They were rather noisy themselves and barely noticed Rudy and Ralph.

The only ones who complained were Sophie the pig and Clarissa the cow. "I need peace and quiet to make milk," Clarissa mooed.

"But Clarissa," Rudy said, "you give milk every day, no matter how loud we are."

"You're keeping me awake every night," Sophie grunted. "I need my beauty sleep."

"Can't argue with that one," Ralph whispered to Rudy.

It was two days before Halloween—time to make costumes for the Halloween Poultry Parade. This caused even more than the usual commotion.

"I'm losing my patience with this uproar," Clarissa bellowed.

"Me too," snorted Sophie, and the two of them went off in a huff.

"What old grumps," Ralph said. "They can't remember what it's like to have fun. I bet they were never young at all."

Rudy felt sorry about bothering Clarissa and Sophie.
He tried to be quiet the whole next day. But when the
animals gathered in the barn that night to finish their
Halloween costumes, he got caught up in the excitement
and added his voice to the squawking.

Suddenly a huge figure rose up in the far corner of the barn, its head almost touching the highest roost. Rudy had never seen a creature so tall. The monster let out a moan as it lurched forward.

The animals tumbled out of the barn in a hurry of feathers. They ran until they reached the top of the hill. Clarissa and Sophie were the slowest runners and the last to arrive, both out of breath.

"What was that thing?" Rudy asked.

"It was the ghost—the poultrygeist," Clarissa gasped.

"The legend says the poultrygeist has been sleeping for a hundred years," whispered Sophie. "I'm afraid you woke it up with your noise."

Nobody dared go back into the barn that night.

When the sun rose the next morning, Rudy and Ralph held each other's beaks closed to keep from crowing. It wasn't easy.

"Did you see that?" Rudy asked when Ralph finally let go of his beak. "The sun came up without us crowing it into the sky."

"Don't tell anybody," Ralph said. "We'll be out of a job."

Everybody stayed out of the barn all day. They even held the Halloween Poultry Parade outside, which was fun because the costumes looked scarier in the dark. But as the night went on, it got colder and colder. One by one, the shivering animals slipped back inside the haunted barn.

Ralph and Rudy were the last ones left outside.
"My drumsticks have turned to Popsicles," Rudy said,
his beak chattering. "Let's go in."
Inside the barn the only sound was snoring.
There was no sign of the poultrygeist.
"Let's pick our roosts. Only two left."

Ralph scanned the rafters, looking for the poultrygeist. "You take the high roost. I'll use this low one next to the exit . . . I mean door."

"No, you should have the highest roost, Ralph. After all, you're taller than me."

"I am not," Ralph yelled. "Look!"

"You're slouching!" Rudy shouted.

Ralph drooped his feathers. "You should have the top roost because you're much handsomer than me."

"No, I'm ugly!" Rudy crowed. "Look!"

"Get up on that top roost!" Ralph hollered.

"No, you get up there!" Rudy screeched.

The two roosters rolled around the floor, feathers flying, when suddenly a shadow fell over them—a very tall shadow.

"Boooooooooooo!" howled the poultrygeist. There was a great flapping and squawking as the animals fled to safety.

But Ralph and Rudy were trapped in a corner.

"Yikes! This is it, buddy," Ralph cried. "We're going to that big roost in the sky."

"Don't give up! We can escape." Rudy grabbed his friend and tried to run around the poultrygeist, but instead the two roosters smacked right into it. And it didn't feel all clammy and ghostlike. Instead it felt like . . .

feed sacks!" Rudy cried. "The poultrygeist is nothing but a bunch of feed sacks all sewn together."

"Can't be!" But Ralph gave a tug on the sacks, and there stood Sophie and Clarissa.

"*Boooooooooooooo!*" Clarissa mooed, her eyes closed.

"Enough with the ghost talk," Sophie said. "We've been unmasked."

"Awesome Halloween costume," Ralph said. "You sure had us fooled."

"They weren't fooling," Rudy said. "They wanted to scare us into being quiet."

"Bingo!" Sophie said. "What gave you the first clue?"

"I don't get it," Ralph said. "I was trying hard to be quiet."

"Not hard enough," said Clarissa.

Later, when the two roosters were alone, Ralph said, "I wasn't really afraid of the poultrygeist, you know."

"Are you kidding?" Rudy squawked. "You were so scared you almost choked on your gizzard!"

"I did not!"

"Did too!"

"Did NOT!"

"DID TOO!"

"Ahem!" said Sophie. "There's more than one way to quiet a pair of rowdy roosters." So she sat on both of them. And the two rowdy roosters remembered that lesson for a long time.